The
Perfect Bear

For Brian, Gabriel and Sasha,
who fill my world with love – *G.S.*

To Lin – *G.B.*

SIMON AND SCHUSTER

First published in Great Britain in 2007 by Simon & Schuster UK Ltd
Africa House, 64-78 Kingsway, London WC2B 6AH
A CBS COMPANY
This paperback edition published in 2008

Text copyright © 2007 Gillian Shields
Illustrations copyright © 2007 Gary Blythe
The right of Gillian Shields and Gary Blythe to be identified as the author
and illustrator of this work has been asserted by them in accordance
with the Copyright, Designs and Patents Act, 1988

Book designed by Genevieve Webster
The text for this book is set in Garamond
The illustrations are rendered in oil paint
All rights reserved, including the right of reproduction in whole or in part in any form

A CIP catalogue record for this book is available from
the British Library upon request

978 1 41691 035 0

Printed in China

1 3 5 7 9 10 8 6 4 2

The Perfect Bear

GILLIAN SHIELDS & GARY BLYTHE

SIMON AND SCHUSTER

London New York Sydney

*T*here was a girl who had a bear, and she was a bit like you.
She was not too big. She was not too small. She was just
somewhere nicely in the middle.

When the bear arrived from the shop, he was very grand.
He had soft white fur, and a little red hat, and a magic key.
When the girl turned the key, the bear sang a song.
He was very proud of his finery and thought he was perfect.

The old pink rabbit, who sat on the chest of drawers, said,

"Hello! What's your name?"

The bear replied haughtily, "My name is Do-Not-Touch."

In the shop, there had been a sign that said,

"DO NOT TOUCH", and the bear thought it was a very good name.

But the girl didn't seem to understand.

She wanted to touch him, and hold him, and play with him.

The bear didn't like this one little bit.

The girl took the bear to the park, but he lost his hat.
She took the bear to the beach, but his fur
became full of sand.

She painted his picture, but accidentally splashed him.

Once, she even left him out in the rain.

The bear was very angry that his white fur was getting dirty.

"Poor Bear!" said the girl one day. "You need a bath."
The Do-Not-Touch bear trembled with fear. The soap stung
his eyes. The pegs pinched his ears. And when he was dry,
his beautiful soft white fur wasn't as white, or soft,
or beautiful as it had been before.

Then something dreadful happened.
When the girl turned his key, there was a
horrible squeaking noise. The bear couldn't sing!
The bath water had ruined his music box.

"Oh dear," said the girl, "I'll have to take it out."
She fetched her doctor's kit.
"Don't worry, Bear," she whispered. "It won't hurt."
"DO NOT TOUCH!" shouted the bear.
But the girl didn't seem to understand.

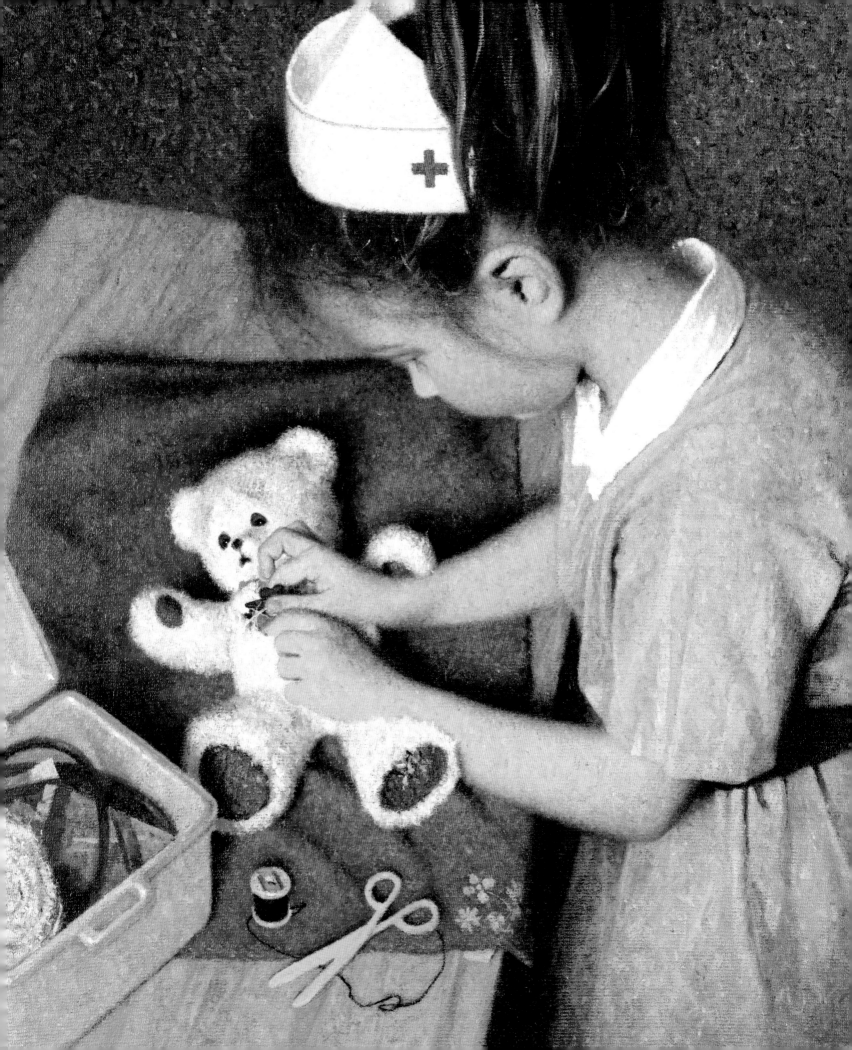

When she had finished, the girl held the bear in front of the mirror.

He saw a small grey reflection, with a hollow place in his middle,

sewn up with big black stitches. The bear sighed.

It didn't matter if people touched him now.

He wasn't a Do-Not-Touch bear any more.

He was just any old bear.

But the girl said a strange thing.

She said, "You're much more cuddly without your music box, Bear."

And she started to take him to bed with her, every night.

The bear liked the night, when no one could see
how shabby he had become.
Every night, the girl held him close and told him stories.
When she fell asleep, the bear would lie awake,
his brown eyes gleaming as if they had tears in them.

The old pink rabbit looked down and asked kindly,

"What's the matter, Bear?"

"I want all my finery back," cried the bear,

"so that everyone will admire me."

"It's much better to be loved than admired, you know,"

said the old pink rabbit.

"What is love?" asked the bear.

"It's what we're all about, little silly," laughed

the old pink rabbit.

"Hats and fur and keys don't matter. They're only on the outside.

It's what is inside us that's important."

"Oh," said the bear, and he tried to think what was inside him,

but he only felt the empty place, where his

music box had been.

The bear started to wonder what was inside the girl.

He noticed that she dressed him warmly if it was cold.

She gave him honey to eat.

She sewed up the hole in his middle when it came apart.

And one night, the girl said softly, "I love you, Bear,"

before falling asleep. But the bear stayed awake all night long, thinking.

The next day, the girl went with her mother to
a big department store. They looked at shoes and suitcases
and saucepans, but when it was time to go home,
the girl said, "I've lost my Bear!"

The girl and her mother looked everywhere.
The bear wasn't near the shoes, or the suitcases, or the saucepans.
He wasn't anywhere. He was lost.
The girl tried not to cry.

In the Lost Property department, a small grey bear was feeling
very strange. He suddenly realised that he wanted to see the girl again,
more than anything in the world. He had the oddest
feeling in the empty place where his old music box had been.
It was … love.

Then the bear saw his girl, running towards him.
She was not too big. She was not too small.
She was just somewhere perfect in the middle.

"I'm so sorry, Bear," said the girl. "I'll never, never
lose you again. Oh, I do love you!"
"I love you too! I love you too!" cried the bear,
trying to make her hear.
And this time, the girl really did understand.

If anyone asks the bear now what he is called, he says,
"My name is Bear. Just Bear."
And the empty place inside him is full of happiness.